# The Toll-Bridge Troll

## Patricia Rae Wolff

### ILLUSTRATED BY

## Kimberly Bulcken Root

Scholastic Inc.

New York  Toronto  London  Auckland  Sydney

ISBN 0-590-97549-8

12 11 10 9 8 7 6 5 4 3 2 1      6 7 8 9/9 0 1/0

Printed in the U.S.A.            08

First Scholastic printing, September 1996

For Jack, of course.
—P. R. W.

To Marian and Herbert Otthofer
for their kindness and prayers.
—K. B. R.

Today was the first day of school, and Trigg didn't want to be late.

He gobbled his breakfast, grabbed his books, and gave his mother a good-bye kiss.

"Have a good day," she said, "and be careful of the troll."

"Yes, Mother," said Trigg.

Trigg walked across the field, up the big hill, and down the long road. When he came to the little bridge, he stopped and looked around.

Just as Trigg stepped onto the rickety wooden bridge, a terrible, ugly troll jumped up from beneath it.

"This is MY bridge!" the troll snarled.
"But I have to cross the bridge to go to school," Trigg said.

"Why?" the troll asked.
"So I can get smart."
"That's not a good reason," the troll said.
"I have to go to school because my mother said so," Trigg said.
"Oh," said the troll. "THAT'S a good reason."

Trigg started across the bridge.

"Wait!" the troll said, jumping in front of Trigg. "This is MY toll bridge. You have to pay a penny to go across."

Trigg thought for a minute. He couldn't pay a penny  every day to go to school. He would just have to trick the troll.

"I have an idea," Trigg said. "We'll ask a riddle. If you answer the riddle, I won't cross your bridge. But if I answer the riddle, I get to cross for free today."

"Oh, goody!" the troll said, jumping up and down. "I like riddles."

"Here's the riddle," Trigg said. "Why does a giraffe have such a long neck?"

The toll-bridge troll hunched down into a thinking crouch. He crunched his face into a thinking frown. *Think. Think. Think. Think.* After a long time, the troll asked, "What's a giraffe?"

"A giraffe is an animal with a long neck," Trigg said.

"Oh." The troll hunched back into his thinking crouch. *Think. Think. Think.*

"I give up," the troll said finally. "Why does a giraffe have such a long neck?"

"Because his head is so far away from his body," Trigg said. "I win! I get to cross for free today!"

The toll-bridge troll stamped his feet. He shook his fists and made awful, angry troll noises. But he let Trigg cross the bridge.

*That worked well*, Trigg thought. *I'll need many more tricky ideas if I'm going to cross the bridge every day without paying.*

After school, the toll-bridge troll was waiting for Trigg.

"My mother  lives under this bridge, too," the troll told Trigg. "She heard your riddle, and she said you tricked me. She said *I* was supposed to ask the riddle."

Trigg just smiled and quickly crossed the bridge. As he ran for home, he stumbled over a hole in the road.

That gave him ⚹ an idea.

The next day, Trigg's mother kissed him good-bye. "Have a good day and be careful of the troll," she said.

"Yes, Mother," said Trigg.

He walked across the field, up the big hill, and down the long road to the bridge. As Trigg stepped onto the bridge, the troll jumped out, looking more terrible than ever.

"This is MY bridge!" the troll snarled.

*Not again*, Trigg thought. "But I have to cross the bridge to go to school," Trigg said.

"Why?"

"So I can get smart."

"That's not a good reason."

"I have to go to school because my mother said so," Trigg said.

"Oh," said the troll. "THAT'S a good reason."

Trigg started across the bridge.

"Wait!" the toll-bridge troll said, and again jumped in front of Trigg. "This is MY toll bridge. You have to pay a penny  to go across."

Trigg pretended to look for money in his pocket. "I don't have a penny," Trigg said. "But I have an idea. Let's ask another riddle. If I answer it, I cross your bridge for free."

OK," said the troll, "but today *I* ask the riddle." He hunched into a thinking crouch. He crunched his face into a thinking frown. *Think. Think. Think. Think.*

After a long time, the troll said, "I don't know any riddles."

"I know one you can use," Trigg said. He whispered it into the troll's ear.

"Oh, that's a good one! How much dirt can you take out of a hole three feet wide and three feet deep?" the troll asked.

Trigg pretended to think. "That's a hard one," he said.

"I win! I win!" the troll shouted. He jumped up and down.

"No, wait!" Trigg said. "Now I remember. The answer is none. There is no dirt in a hole."

The troll stamped his feet. He shook his fists and made awful, angry troll noises.

*I hope I don't run out of riddles*, Trigg thought as he ran across the bridge.

After school, the troll was waiting for Trigg.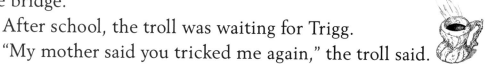

"My mother said you tricked me again," the troll said. "She said you knew the answer when you told me the riddle to use."

Could be," Trigg said, quickly crossing the bridge. As he ran for home, he spied two coins lying in the dirt on the road ahead.

That gave him  an idea.

The next day, Trigg's mother kissed him good-bye, told him to have a good day, and warned him to watch out for the troll.

"Yes, Mother," Trigg said.

Trigg could see the troll waiting for him, looking more ugly than ever.

"This is MY bridge!" the troll snarled.

Trigg took a deep breath. "But-I-have-to-cross-the-bridge-to-go-to-school-to-get-smart-because-my-mother-said-so," he said.

"Oh, that's right. Now I remember."

Trigg started across the bridge.

"Wait!" the troll said. "This is MY toll bridge. You have to pay a penny to go across."

Trigg sighed. "I have another ⊙ idea."

"No more riddles," the troll said. "My mother's mad at me because of your riddles."

No riddles," Trigg said. He reached into his pocket. "I have six cents," he told the toll-bridge troll. "If you can guess what kinds of coins they are, I'll give them all to you. I'll even tell you how many coins I have to make the six cents."

"It's a deal! My mother's going to be proud of me this time," the troll said. "I'm good at money."

"I have two coins," Trigg said, "and one of them isn't a nickel."

"You have six cents with only two coins, and one of them isn't a nickel," the troll repeated.

"Right."

The toll-bridge troll hunched into his thinking crouch. He crunched his face into his thinking frown. *Think. Think. Think. Think.*

"I give up," the troll said after a long while.

Trigg opened his hand. There was one nickel and one penny.

"But you said one of them wasn't a nickel," the troll said.

"Right," said Trigg. He picked up the penny and held it up. "This one isn't a nickel." Trigg ran across the bridge.

After school, the troll was waiting for Trigg.

"My mother said you tricked me again," the troll said.

Trigg just smiled.

You know what else my mother said?"

"What?" asked Trigg.

"She said tomorrow I have to go to school with you. So I can get smart."

*Walk to school each day with a terrible, ugly troll? Oh well,* Trigg thought with a sigh, *at least I won't have to pay the toll!*